CW00801530

Our Isolated Dale

Writing from Weardale

for our friend,

Jenny Spooner

Proceeds from the sale of this anthology
will be donated to local Covid-19 charities

Acknowledgements

NorthPens would like to thank the Weardale Area Action Partnership Covid-19
Assistance Fund for supporting the creation of this anthology and the associated film, *Our Isolated Dale*

Published by NorthPens, Weardale, Co. Durham, 2021
www.northpens.com
northpens15@gmail.com

Text © individual writers
All photographs © Marie Gardiner and Lonely Tower Film & Media
Cover design: Kate Hall Design

ISBN: 978-1-8384481-0-3

Book design and printing: Lintons Printers Ltd,
3E & 3F Castle Close Industrial Estate, Crook, County Durham DL15 8LU

Foreword

Our Isolated Dale has two incarnations, as a film and now a book. Unable to hold our regular weekly meetings at Stanhope Community Centre during this last turbulent and uncertain year, NorthPens Writers nonetheless carried on writing and getting together via Zoom.

Working alongside local authors Avril Joy, Phil Mews and Wendy Robertson, we created a collection of poems, stories and anecdotes reflecting what it has been like to experience lockdown in Weardale. Everybody's take on the situation was different, but there was a common need to find a creative outlet for our feelings and to record our experiences. Now that so much of our cultural life has gone on-line, making a film based on our writing was the obvious thing to do. Acclaimed local film producers, *Lonely Tower Film & Media*, worked with NorthPens to produce a wonderful short film, a totally new venture for the group, way outside our comfort zone, challenging but immensely rewarding.

This anthology represents the next phase of the project. The work collected for the film *Our Isolated Dale* has been added to and is complemented by Marie Gardiner's evocative photographs. Inevitably, most of what you will read has been informed by our experiences of living in a remote dale during a pandemic, difficult times but times recorded with resilience and humour.

Chris Powell, March 2021

NorthPens is a community writers' group based in Stanhope, Weardale. As well as producing their own work, its members host open workshops and masterclasses with professional writers, run workshops in schools, a childrens' writing competition and the annual Weardale WordFest. Further information: www.northpens.com or email: northpens15@gmail.com

Links to the film, *Our Isolated Dale* can be found on the NorthPens website.

Contents

Mothers' Day 21/3/20 - Lockdown is Coming

Walking up to Sedling Vein, lungs burst,
snatching at pure air blowing off Middlehope Moor,
we stop. Drinking in the view,
aching legs ease,
all tiredness disperses to the far horizon.
Hear the curlews returning to nest,
see the deer racing up steep fields
through tumbling stone walls.
At this very moment I want to
wrap the world in cotton wool,
soft muslin sheets,
anything,
anything to keep it safe.

Susan Nicholson

When it is time to Breathe, Breathe, and Make Postcards

Lately only the small things
an admiration for the stitching of gowns
check out Instagram @fionasews
#fortheloveofscrubs

donations welcome no matter how small,
making dinner for 'the gentleman next door.'
Window for a mask

lately I live in hawthorn
fattened with wood pigeon,
a squabble of sparrows at my chest,

in the driest April on record I water
the tulip pots, drift in the catch breath
of broken nights,

across a field of years
to golden saxifrage, opposite-leaved
and summer on a mossy heath,

Sundays walking in Kentish apple
orchards, island Greece, spitting stones
from black kalamata olives.

Lately only the small things

breath, postcards, scraps of torn
paper, put back together, renga
an attempt to retrieve.

There are too many pictures of food
to scroll through for my liking,
too many briefings,

the world is numberless
in its grief, all our houses burning,
one way or another, hunger.

Lately, only the small things

next door's magnolia opening
like a wound, flesh falling
breath on stone

I imagine eating only blackcurrants
my grandmother's pastry
swollen fingers sifting flour to bowl

pale blossom in the wind
rising and falling
like a lung.

Avril Joy

20/20 A Vision for the Future

I've been saving my sanity
keeping safe by not looking deep
giving myself hard physical tasks
to see me through from one day to the next
one week
one month
two
three
four

the greenhouse decluttered, debugged
declared ready
seeded
potted on
and on
growing

the shed unburied
tins emptied, sorted, refilled, labeled
returned to shelves newly regimented

father's armchair stripped back to skeletal frame
rewebbed, restuffed, reupholstered, reborn.

the 20/20 garden dug clay deep... a vision for the future
ground elder
creeping honeysuckle
bramble
couch
a netty's worth of bricks
removed, replaced by
salad greens
legumes
squash
and herbs

kitchen cupboards built
doors painted 50's revival

and still I stay safe
shallow
and safe

and deep in the night
my hip cries out
'What about me?
Save me.'

Eve Stocks

Slow Down

A musty old folder weathered with age,
the long faded ink as I study the page,
my mother's handwriting and beautiful script
the poems are falling, they drop from her lips.
But she is long gone, and I wouldn't have known
that lockdown gave time and the freedom of home.

I hurried and scurried in a pre-Covid life,
but now I draw breath and don't have the strife
so I read the old poems with dust on the page,
the smell of the leather so battered with age

Will I go back? It's quite hard to say
this frenetic world seems so far away.

Julia Organ

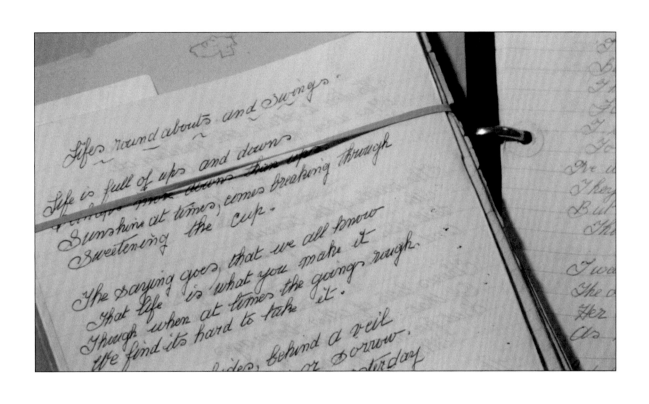

Lifes round abouts and swings.

Life is full of ups and downs
Sunshine at times, comes breaking through
Sweetening the cup.

The saying goes, that we all know
That life is what you make it
Though when at times the going rough.
We find its hard to take it.

behind a veil
Sorrow
sterday

Normal

Life changes
moment by moment
evolving
slow and inconspicuous
unnoticed
then comes
pandemic
panic
pandemonium
fractured normality
humanity interrupted
eyes darting
alert for danger
as if becoming deer
scuttling sideways
to avoid others
as if becoming crab
going to ground
remaining indoors
as if becoming mole
survival of the fittest
the youngest
as if becoming animal
once again
under the sway
of the old god
Pan

Sara Parker-Fuller

Angle Grinder

Eight in the morning. Leaf shadows flicker over teacup. Look – a robin! Suddenly a high-pitched scream slices the air, spins noise through the sky...on and on, out into the blue, a string stretched taut to infinity. Peace returns. A thoughtful sip. Who is having work done? Open book. And again, the squeal of metal drilling the air, teeth on edge now, the silence torn.

Retreat indoors. Fragrance of wood smoke and tea. Through the window, sun is slanted on angled roof tops, ochre tiles bright. But still the distant shriek whines its way into my sanctuary, grinding down all hope of a quiet awakening. Woodsmoke harsh now, tea metallic against tongue, blade against stone, against metal, against bone. A sudden quiet. An apprehensive breath. Done? No – one more scalpel screed across plate, fingernails scraped down blackboard, dragged across cheekbones, jabbed into eye sockets ...

No, not that. Do something. Into the dark kitchen. Chop fruit. Apples cool, green. Knife thumps on wood, counterpoint to the incessant keening that now prods the sore places, heart clenched, fists rammed into pockets, pacing the floor as fruit browns, my head sliced into segments, my heart crying out for a truce...and on and on and on, out into the bleached places of my mind, tundra stretched tight under ashen sky, sun glare white in the tensioned air.

A distant bell chimes. A gentle surge of calm rolls over the land, silent music. Water trickles over fingers, scent of rose. Bread is broken. The day turns sweetly on its hinge.

Maggi Deimel

Slow

There is magic in these times of enforced retreat
perhaps it was always there
but we were too busy to notice
time stretches and contracts
reshaping things in strange ways
silver has appeared at my temples
a sense that the crone days aren't too far away
wisdom inhabits this stillness
joy hangs in the silence
the world exists in a one-mile radius
as if a long-forgotten age has returned
everything is simple
I plant seeds and delight in their slow progress
only the bees are busy now

Sara Parker-Fuller

Lockdown Calendar

March 2020. The kitchen calendar: a breathless tangle of engagements, reminders, commitments, things that needed to be done, pencilled in weeks ahead. Week three: under siege, empty shops, a diagonal stripe scrawled through every day. Cancelled. Postponed. Pencilled out. Dates flying off the page like meteorites, crashing into the life you thought you could take for granted, leaving a scatter pattern of scars and desolate fires burning on the wall.

In April, the death toll peaked and the days flattened. Laid out like a jigsaw. Patterned: collect prescriptions, queue at the Co-op, one bag for us, one for Trevor. That's the morning gone. Conversations are like gems, snatched out of the ground, with people you barely know. Are you finding things to do? Aren't we lucky we live here? Have you tidied the cupboards? Stay safe. The pause button had been pressed, but, even in lockdown, life is not long enough to steam clean the toaster.

We were treading water, looking at the sky. But in May, pieces of the jigsaw fell out. Bare places where people used to be. Days defined by boxes: delivery boxes, faces in boxes on a screen. People boxed in by their doorways, clapping as the nights grow shorter. And you walk, and walk and walk in the heat and think, yes, I'm glad I live here. Furtive strangers appear on the high fells. Refugees returning to their roots, to a place that seems, somehow, safer. Until the slogans change, the floodgates left ajar, and nowhere feels safe.

June was a long month. Pockmarked by worry, no pattern, no jigsaw, still the boxes. Punctured by anxious telephone calls, the parameters become treacherous, like an electric fence hidden in the long grass. Rules only apply to those who need rules. Jean leaves a Webb's lettuce and gooseberry jam on the wheelie bin. Lights come back on in the Travel Agent's. The whole world demands a refund. You feel the circulation return to your frozen fingers; it's a relief to see the blood come back but, my god, it hurts!

And in July, you look back. Lives are frail, but life is strong. Four small months sticking up out of the hills like dinosaur bones. Today, there was another funeral, another fossil trace, a footprint in the sand. The Spring was another country, one you struggle to remember. In April, you were glad to be here, cocooned by isolation. You walked freely, everything you needed was within your grasp, the unseen web across your corner of the land was a safety net, and not a trap.

Chris Powell

Encounter with Sainsbury's

I went shopping for the first time in four months. I felt like a novice
in a strange world. Queuing? No love, you can go straight in at this hour.
Do I look that old? Oh vanity! Face masks? Some do, most don't, but they
are so uncomfortable and not designed to fit with hearing aids, and a
friend has already lost one of hers. New layout? Shelves and aisles
changed and re-ordered. No love, you'll find jams at the bottom of the
next aisle. Check out? Claustrophobic barriers to separate me from
other people and the woman at the till. Contactless cards? No love, you
need to hold it just there. How many idiots like me has she had to
initiate, patiently, into this new world of what used to be ordinary shopping?

Jo Cundy

Rituals and Habits

My morning ritual remains unchanged, except that I now have nowhere to go, and nothing to rise for. I now have day pyjamas, and sleep pyjamas. I really would not bother, but the neighbours might see me whilst I'm pegging out washing, and need some sign that I have not become a total slob. My toilette has always been of the 'wash and go' school. No change there, then. We take it in turns to push the Dyson around in a desultory fashion, one glaring at the other if they feel that they have sacrificed more Dyson time, or moved an item of furniture. There are extra brownie points for this. I found a squeaky mouse under a sofa, and the cat has only been dead since February.

Lunch has ceased to exist. In my world, it has become a part of breakfast, and him indoors needs feeding every couple of hours, no matter what. I have no one to bake for, I cannot give food away in case it has added Covid, and we are both trying to diet for our next jolly, which has been cancelled three times to date. I go hopefully around the world with Jane, Rick, and Bettany's cleavage. She really would make a magnificent figurehead, would Bettany. Not sure of her aerodynamics though - it would take the wind a while to negotiate her headland.

Afternoons are spent watching our individual TV programmes. I refer to his programmes as 'rubbish'

He calls mine 'shite'. I started out lockdown with the intent to read a lot and to create wonderful written works. That lasted around two days, or when I was notified that the first holiday had been cancelled. I have sulked ever since. Shopping is also a ritual. He drives to the shop. I go in, spray the trolley, purchase the food, pack it and pay. Shopping is much heavier since lockdown. I find that I am purchasing a lot of bottled products. There has to be some way that the contents can be considered as part of our five a day. Well, in my world, anyway.

Judy Goodwin

The Ritual of the Fragrant Leaf

She boils the kettle, warms the pot, pours the hot water onto the tea leaves (she is a purist), and waits for it to brew. This early morning cup of tea is the one fixed point, the one ritual, left unchanged in her life. Daily walks to shops or friends, drives out in the car, trips to concerts, films or theatres – all have gone, sacrificed to lockdown. The hours, the days, the weeks, have all lost their structure and even meals have become indeed moveable feasts. She ponders whether those working from home and maintaining a semblance of office routine, or those endeavouring to keep children to some sort of school timetable, have the advantage of imposed structure. Whereas she, on her own, had settled into an active retirement organised around friends and family, hobbies and interests. And now? Now there are no necessary tasks, no pressing commitments, no need to consult the diary and plan the day at this early hour. Instead, she has been working on the challenge of finding new routines, new structures, new creative options. And being in the house all day the afternoon cup of tea is becoming a new fixed ritual ... ah now . . . different teapot? Different tea?

Jo Cundy

The Corned Beef Chronicles

Week 1

'It won't come up the Dale,' said the woman outside the paper shop. She must have heard about the magic Covid repelling barrier at Harperley Bank, I thought. 'It's just the media hyping it all up.' She continued with a confidence that made me wonder for a moment if she had inside knowledge of the virus.

That morning, I sat down with my coffee and made a shopping list, after turning down the volume on the telly. Piers Morgan's face was puce with rage. He's always upset about something. Graphics bounced around on the screen telling us the death toll in Italy before it cut to the Prime Minister. Boris didn't seem too bothered about the virus. I think he expects us all to be terribly British about it and not make a fuss.

I was starting to worry. My husband's a nurse so, naturally, I was concerned about him going to work but actually this morning I was more anxious about not being able to buy enough corned beef. I don't even like the stuff. What would I want with four tins of corned beef? If this is the end of civilisation as we know it, surely I can rustle up a meal without resorting to corned beef? There's talk of toilet roll shortages and rationing. Why is everyone queuing outside Morrisons at 6 in the morning for bloody bog roll?

Work called. They are letting everyone go. There was talk of something called 'furlough' which I'd never heard of. How do I tell Martin? He's got enough on his plate at the hospital.

I put the news on again. They're going to build a bloody great big hospital in London. It's going to be so big they describe its size in terms of football pitches. I'm none the wiser. What do I know about football pitches?

Week 2

'Social distancing' – that's another new phrase we keep hearing. We've to avoid contact with other people. That's how it spreads, apparently.

Work called back. Apparently, they can't furlough me. Not sure how I can tell Martin. No money. How will I pay the mortgage? More to the point, what am I going to do about the bloody corned beef? We're down to two tins.

I walk along the streets and the windows are filled with rainbows.

We clapped last night for the NHS. That's the royal we. Martin was on his way home and drove through the village as people lined the streets. I think he was touched, he doesn't say a lot. 'Just be thankful you weren't in the back of a hearse,' I said thinking of Princess Diana.

'As long as they remember when it comes to dishing out pay rises,' he said, 'they can clap all they want.' I know he's not holding his breath.

Week 3

I queued outside the paper shop this morning. I didn't want a paper but I'd heard that they had some corned beef in stock. There was one small tin left. £2.68. I paid without saying anything. That's three tins in the cupboard. I felt guilty. Am I hoarding? I made a large corned beef and potato pie and left half on my brother's doorstep to alleviate the guilt. I rang the bell and stepped so far back I almost fell into the road in the path of a Range Rover. That's 'social distancing' for you.

Week 6

I'm over the corned beef now. We've managed to get a mortgage holiday without any shame. Piers is still very angry in the mornings. They've been short of PPE at the hospitals so people are making it at home. Martin's face is sore and red. He looks like he's dipped his flannel in the deep fat fryer. I'm not working yet. I feel useless and helpless. It's actually upsetting me more than this wretched virus. Stop it, now I'm being selfish.

Week 12

A card came in the post. 'Happy Lockdown Birthday!' it said, rather too cheerily. I'm fifty. I'm still here I tell myself and that gives me some comfort. Others aren't so lucky.

Auntie Brenda 'phoned, she's discovered Netflix at the age of 82 and is now an avid fan of Breaking Bad. What's wrong with Escape to the Country? The thought of my octogenarian Aunt watching someone cooking meth in a motor home makes me laugh. Perhaps that's what she meant when she said it reminded her of her time as a dinner lady.

Week 20

The pubs are going to reopen. People are weary. They look weary, their voices are weary. The thought of having a beer with a friend gives them hope. Yes, a socially-distanced beer!

We've stopped clapping now. It was wearing very thin by the end and if I had to witness one more girl having a crack at Titanic with a karaoke machine outside her nana's nursing home, I'd have chucked a bucket of water over her, socially distanced of course!

Week... I've lost count ...

Changes are afoot. New job waiting for me to start. Martin's PPE rashes have gone. The pubs are open. People are taking small brave steps out there. In the streets the rainbows in the windows have faded a little. There is less talk of heroes now but, perhaps ironically, everyone is wearing masks.

Week 46

100,000 people have died from the virus. One hundred thousand! People are arguing on social media. Society feels divided. The NHS is still battling on day in, day out. Martin gets on with it and doesn't complain. I think everyone is done in now. I keep thinking about those poor grieving families. As for me, I'm remaining positive. After all, I've still got one tin of corned beef left.

Phil Mews

The New Normal

The English language has always had a penchant for pinching words from other languages, euphemistically known as 'loan words', assigning new meaning to old words (not necessarily dropping the original meaning in the process), turning nouns into verbs, creating new conjuncts and so on. English people used to joke that we did it to confuse the foreigners.

This is accelerated during significant events such as the two world wars, the space race or the growth of the internet. At the moment the Covid-19 pandemic is creating a field day for wordsmiths world-wide.

Go back just a few months and how many people would have known what an air-bridge was? Or what the 'R' Rate indicated? Or what social distancing meant? To deep-clean probably inferred the carpet was very dirty and bubbles came in little tubes for kids to blow.

To take bubbles as an example: in Elizabeth Von Arnim's novel 'The Enchanted April', Mrs Wilkins observes 'that people could only be really happy in pairs – any sorts of pairs'. If she had lived 100 years later, she may very well have used the word 'bubbles'.

So there is now a whole raft of new and changed words and phrases at our disposal. We have become so used to them that, when used in their old sense, they can cause momentary confusion. We can spin entire paragraphs with them, for example: if one's bubble was unfortunate enough to jump on an air-bridge to a country that suddenly goes into lockdown because its 'R' rate spikes (possibly due to lack of enforcement of social distancing) then, on return, one's bubble would have to self-isolate for fourteen days because this is the new normal.

And Mrs Wilkins, sitting on her chair in San Salvatore 100 years ago, while understanding all the words and phrases, wouldn't have a clue what you were talking about.

Mike Kane

Silent Britain

Britain is silent in the sunshine today,
spring has sprung but there's no-one to see.
Jackdaws take over the roads,
no-one sees the new twin lambs touch noses
or the wobbly calves lean on their mothers.
The daffodils are blooming to themselves
and the waysides in the woods
are rustling alone.

The thrum of motorcycles has gone,
replaced by birdsong and the hum of lawnmowers
as people do as they are asked and stay at home,
the occasional clink of glass
hitting the recycle bin is followed by the pop
of its successor.
One a.m. is the new bedtime
delayed by another glass of wine.

Are you awake yet? You should be.
Along the lane, walking just past dawn
nature's broadcasts are louder than TVs.
So stop, listen! Can you hear them?
The curlew's cry curves upward,
ponderously lifting us out of
cold winds and dark skies.
A flutter and flutter of twittering
swoops over our heads as
the swallows return,
and somewhere, echoing unseen,
the cuckoo's sparse notes.
And then be still, hush,
so you may catch the rising spirit of
summer on its way,
promised to us in the music
of a skylark.
Be still. Listen.
Sometimes it takes our silence
for us to hear.

Geri Poole, Judy Goodwin, Susan Nicholson

The Door

Before lockdown, a walk was always for a purpose: walking the dog, heading for a destination (i.e. The Grey Bull), getting out of the house with grandchildren addicted to their phones and games.

And then a walk became a walk, something to be enjoyed, a gentle stroll watching the wildlife. In Ashes Quarry there are two pairs of nesting moorhens, a colony of mallards and two very large fish, usually visible early morning. The mine road on Crawleyside, known locally as the Rully Way, is another favourite walk. I have enjoyed walking this route for over forty years, but this year my husband came too and we have taken more time to look at the flowers and plants and to learn their names. We could hear the birds more clearly without the background traffic noise. Butterflies, dragonflies, grasshoppers and insect life abounded. We saw deer, squirrels, rabbits and a slow-worm, which neither of us had seen before. We clambered into another quarry to inspect the frog pond and monitor the frogspawn.

Further along the road is yet another quarry face with a frog pond at the base. It is hugely overgrown, and while we could hear the frogs we couldn't see them. So I tried to find another access point. Walking through the trees, I could see a path and a clearing ahead. The path led me to the quarry face and at its base there was a door with a slanting girder acting as a kind of lintel. The door was green and had what looked like windows cut into it. My husband was born in the village in an era when we all roamed more freely and he had never seen the door before.

The door fascinated me and I would have loved to get closer, but the area above looked unstable. The place looked as if it should belong to a hobbit or some subterranean creature who shies away from human company.

The truth is obviously more prosaic. It was the entrance to a mine shaft that had been deemed dangerous and therefore the entry was blocked, not roughly like a lot of the entrances along there, but with a custom made door. I am sure if I looked in I would see nothing but earth and stones, but I prefer to furnish it in my imagination.

Katy Wallace

Birds

Birds keep coming into our house now it's lockdown. A bunch of friendly sparrows has been coming into the garden for a few years now. They tolerate us when we are outside in their territory, only flapping away when a louder than usual noise makes us all jump.

The newcomers, the friendly fearless newcomers, are blackbirds and thrushes. They hop around our feet or sneak up behind us, whooshing past our ears on their way home. One even landed on the glass table outside, where I was eating risotto. If I'd stayed still he would have eaten off my plate. I nearly let him, but decided, as we are all isolating because of the virus, maybe not. Can blackbirds carry a virus? I think they may.

So, we have two pairs of birds, two blackbirds and two thrushes. They grace us with their presence every day. We do feed them, of course, but then we have done for years. It's the virus: it's changed everything. Birds have lost their fear of us, we are just part of the furniture. Recently, they have started wandering about inside. Not just the porch, but the kitchen. Can they smell food? Can they smell any way?

This morning, one of the blackbirds took a step too far. We were busy and did not see him hopping around on the kitchen carpet until, suddenly startled, he flew straight at the kitchen window, knocked himself out and dropped upside down into my cleaning container. I took the whole lot outside, tipped everything onto the flags, wrapped him in the dishcloth and laid him under the butterfly bush. I thought he was a goner.

A few minutes later his partner appeared flying rapidly around the garden, looking concerned. Eventually she spotted him, waited till we went back inside and hopped down next to him. She stayed with him, touching him with her beak. He sat up. After a while they flew off together, going back home.

No-one is ever going to tell me that birds do not express affection for one another. Not after that lovers' tryst beneath the butterfly bush.

Geri Poole

Trees

A Bishop Auckland garden in lockdown -
found in a notebook written in October 2002
developed March 2020

Green light drips onto sooty bark
the white sun forges pathways
onto petals of yellow aconite
spotlighting chunky bluebells
awakened from their ancient bulbs.

Raw branches push outwards and up
escaping the broad trunk -
a descendant of the ancient woodland
rooted here, predating the existence of
the main street this whole town,

its straight road echoing with
the tramp-tramp of mercenary feet
pacing the land, holding it in thrall
for an emperor lounging now
in glimmering Mediterranean light.

Now the child walks through the trees,
trailing her hand on the roughened bark.
She puts her face to the sky and savours
the pearls of rain that drop onto her round
brow, into her closed eye.

Wendy Robertson

Anniversary

Darkness. Milk of the moon is tipped
through trees.
Mother's kindness fills the fields.

Soft thread of footsteps through dry grass
so far outside
my comfort zone I cannot fall further.

This is the spot on which we lay
shoulder to shoulder
secret marks of beauty on a vellum page.

Ferns creep intricate up the hill
through myriad masks I glimpse
glint of Dionysius.

But now, now is the time of burial.
Quiet waters cover the moon's face
again
and I must wait
hung between earth and sky
again.

Maggi Deimel

Lockdown

From Crawley Incline over Bashaw Rigg
the gamekeeper's track wanders up the moor,
today's escape from lockdown's iron grip
and the dream-world of these sleepwalking days.
Up here permitted daily exercise
means freedom and a chance to breathe clean air.
A cool breeze gently combs the heather and
whispers through the walls of the old sheep fold.
The moors create their own social distance.

It is breeding season for upland birds;
curlews glide effortlessly across the moor
murmuring their soft and wistful love-weep
while lapwings wheel and dive in mad display,
bleeping like strange demented aliens.
We climb to the summit of Collier Law
where, drawing our breath, we stop to survey
the broad sweep of the dale spread out below.
The land dreams in sleep beneath the heat haze
of a warm, dry spring no-one expected,
and untroubled by human contagion
the lowland trees are thrusting into leaf,
eager to embrace an early summer.

Leaving behind our silent reflections
we follow Black Burn to make a descent
where tetchy red grouse urge us to 'go back'
and small heath butterflies basking in heat
scoot away to avoid our tramping feet.
By the time we reach Shittlehope we are
thinking of home and what waits for us there.
The daily briefing and the new death toll,
the current R-number, *Clap for Carers*,
the liturgy of nightmares still to come
that haunt our subconscious pandemic dreams.

What sustains us through these darkest of days
is our connection to the airy moors,
that upper world of sunlight, wind and rain
where Nature's cycle turns the wheel of life,
regardless of our self-inflicted woes.
We too are children of this world although
in our hubris we often do forget.
These troubled times remind us of the need
to slow down, slacken our pace, and stop;
hear once again that deeper, ancient pulse
that drives a living world in harmony.
In darkness we can sow the seeds of hope
but all must strive to bring them to the light.

Stay at home
But stay tuned
Work to restore the balance
Save lives.

Mike Powell

Winter

Cold stare of winter
sombre charcoal skies
chilled boisterous air
dank dreary months of stagnant gloom
sharp rain will hide behind a winter veil
as we give thanks when floods don't reach our door
spring's softer fall will gently quench the earths dry soil.
as floods abate
and those poor souls reclaim their homes again.

Julia Organ

Please Notice Me

Oh can you share some chat with me,
and smile and laugh at this or that?
I nod hello! (is that the key?)
Oh can you share some chat with me?
You pass me by, so you can see
I am alone, in window sat,
so can you share some chat with me,
and smile and laugh at this or that?

Susan Nicholson

Ely Rigby

Ely Rigby lives nearby. Pale and insubstantial. Can't invite him over for a coffee and a cake. It's the lockdown. It's truly locked him down. He peers out, door half open, well back from the grocery boy. Shuts the door quickly.

This time is too much for some people. All the unfortunate characteristics of old age are shining too bright: white hair thinning, curved back, gnarled fingers, low weedy voice. He used to crack jokes with his neighbours, pub every night, swing his little granddaughter around. She loved it. Haven't seen them in months. Maybe it's too painful to see him through a crack in the door. She wouldn't understand.

Indoors he is caught by ghosts in hidden corners, silent, persistent, unshakeable. Too quiet, the tread of carpet slippers. Too much, the constant turning in the creaking bed, the sadness in the night. Is it Death at the door, coughing gently, smiling and cheerful, holding out a bag of oranges?

Geri Poole

Fred's Remembrance

10.45 a.m. Fred walks slowly up the garden path. The greenhouse is quiet now, new growth and fulsomeness have ended. He slides open the door and steps inside, breathing in the chilled, earthy air.

Fred has never accepted his medals and wouldn't dream of marching in a parade following banners, standards and the great and good of the town.

'Do you think it's a party, an event to show off, a bit of a do? Have you no real respect?' This is his reply when invited each and every year by the Council to the local Remembrance service at the War Memorial. Fred had fought for his family, his community, not some stuck-up monarch or some politician's idea about what a country should do.

10.55 a.m. Fred straightens the muffler round his neck, takes off his cap, places his arms at his side and remembers...

He remembers Jonny Top Shop, Idwal, the twins Bob and Frank, Vaughan Middle Farm and Davey Chapel House. Fred remembers their riverbank swing, their muddy shorts, grass stained knees, and bramble scratched hands. He remembers their picnics, jam and bread, scrumped apples, and, if they were lucky, a slice of home pressed tongue left over from Sunday's tea. He remembers their Mams standing on Bank Top calling for them to, 'Come in now, it's getting late.'

And then, and then...he remembers when suddenly the Mams had no one to call in. They had still been boys, barely young men, but had swapped the brambles and mud slide for barbed wire and the filthy mud of trenches. No more did he hear their names being called home.

11.05 a.m. Fred steps out of the greenhouse. A wren darts through the withered branches, then stops and sings. Well, thinks Fred, that's finer than the Last Post in my book, and he wipes away a tear.

Susan Nicholson

Being Noel Murless

My brother always wanted to be a bus driver or conductor, anything to do with buses. One Christmas, our parents tracked down a bus conductor outfit and I had to spend Christmas afternoon boarding and disembarking from imaginary buses, while my brother dispensed tickets and change from his Setrite machine and cash satchel combo. Thus started my brother's lifelong obsession with the transport industry, and my role as unwilling destination blind roller-outer.

I, on the other hand, wanted to be Noel Murless, a famous racehorse trainer of the time. My mother blamed my father's mother, who used to wheel me in my pushchair to illegal bookmakers.

I never could understand the shortage of books at these places, usually someone's smoky back kitchen. Grandma said that it was our secret and she would take me to Aunty Glad's shop for sweets afterwards. All my father's immediate family loved horse racing. Whenever any of them came to stay, they would spend a day at Manchester Racecourse. They always took my brother with them, to my utter disgust. He would spend the day in the coach park, recording bus numbers, while I stayed at home, fuming.

The logistics of being Noel Murless in a suburban setting did not faze me. The garage could become a stable and there was a fine public park nearby to exercise my horses in. My parents could supply the hay, straw and feed. I would need to source a hairy ginger tweed jacket and a battered trilby hat and would have to learn to be a heavy smoker, like my hero. My parents smoked, which I hated, so this would require some negotiation. Perhaps Mr Murless might give up smoking? I had thought about ways to attract a number of multi-millionaire owners, would Hallwood Avenue be glamorous enough for Mr Joel and the Sassoons? Sixty horses would take up a lot of space and the neighbours might complain about the smell. I also, at this point, didn't ride. A minor detail.

So the year of my eleventh birthday saw me and my friends, Julia and Gillian, make our way by bus to Prestwich, and Miss Hilda Swift's riding academy - a group of pit stables and assorted outbuildings, set in a muddy field. Hilda herself did not ride, because of allergies, but her 'friend', Beryl, did. I was allocated a piebald Clydesdale horse called Clynette, as my weight issues and lack of coordination required her reinforced frame. Hilda stood in the centre, with a 'How to Ride for Dummies' in her hands, while we practiced rising trots and gripping with our thighs. Beryl was our life class model and Hilda did the voiceover. We would then go for a ride through Prestwich's finest, Hilda walking alongside, sharing nuggets of her great riding experience and end with a canter, if we were lucky. I was aware that my riding style resembled a sack of potatoes, and that, game as I was, I was never going to be Noel Murless.

Judy Goodwin

Travel

Jim And Sally pour themselves a glass of wine and consider where they could visit. Of course, the Greek Islands are their favourite destination, but, as that is not possible, they settle in front of the television to see what their options are tonight. First, a trip to New Zealand for an episode of *Wanted Down Under*. Majestic mountains or relaxed living on the coast? Nice to look at, but not to live in they agreed.

Or they could catch up with Rick Stein on his journey from Venice to Istanbul. This week, he is in Turkey. A fascinating country, a melting pot between two continents and surely a place to put on the bucket list. Tonight he is cooking grilled mackerel stuffed with hot red pepper paste, parsley and garlic. Definitely one to try!

They could stay in the Mediterranean, join Ainsley Harriott on a 44 foot catamaran, imagine the breeze and warm sun on their faces as the boat heads for the shore and another fish dish. They pour another glass of wine, remembering boat trips in Spain and Greece, some more successful than others. A near disaster off the coast of Ibiza, for example, when the captain had taken them too close to the rocky shore and seemed to have difficulty turning. One Spanish woman had taken out her rosary beads and started praying. That didn't reassure them. They did get back safely, but the captain was receiving a lot of abuse from the Spanish passengers so they left them to it and headed to a bar for a much needed drink.

Next, they're off to the southern hemisphere again in the company of Griff Rhys Jones as he reports on the work of Dr Julian Fennesey and his mission to save an endangered species of giraffe. Fascinating.

And then it's back to Britain for a history lesson on Lake Vrynwy, a large reservoir in Powys, and a visit to the National Botanic Gardens of Wales before another trip to the Spanish coast. They're in Valencia this time where local estate agent, Scarlett Douglas, is helping a couple look for their ideal a holiday home.

For a complete change of mood and scenery, Simon Reeves takes them to Alaska to witness the effect of climate change in the Denali National Park. And the journeys are not over yet! They could join the teams in Panama City as they begin their *Race Across the World*, or accompany Joanna Lumley to Guantanamo before heading with her to The Windward Pass in Haiti. The bucket list gets ever longer.

Lockdown will not last forever, it just feels like it. Get out the holiday snaps and plan the next one. Jim and Sally know where they are going.

Katy Wallace

Lockdown Blues

I've got the lockdown blues
fed up with Covid news,
my staycation vacation
is no consolation
when I want Catalonian views!

Mike Kane

On the Hill

A lockdown dream. One of those intricate, logical dreams that make no sense at all when you wake up. It was the landscape she remembered, although it looked nothing like the landscape she remembered. Nonetheless, even recalling the dream is a bonus, at her age.

She dresses carefully, like you do when you're off to visit an elderly relative you've not seen for a while. Linen Capri pants, white, fresh pressed, the leopard skin vest and matching ballet flats, her mother's gold hoop earrings. She takes Ted a cup of tea.

'You're driving,' she says.

He grunts, 'Too hot.'

'Too hot to stay here. We need some air.'

The town is deserted when they drive through. Clammy, dusty, litter blowing in the gutters. Nothing new. It has always been like that, minus the heat. Tumbleweed and steel shutters on Friday nights.

'Is this it?' Ted stares out of the window in disbelief. 'I'm not walking down there.' He gets out of the car, extracts a folding chair from the boot and settles himself by the side of the road in the sunshine. 'There's nowt here!'

She points to a row of cottages on the skyline, 'It's where I grew up, look, up there!'

He looks at the terrain, the tussock grass, the interlocking hillocks, the steep stony track, the sheep. He looks at her feet. 'You'll not get far in those shoes.'

She used to run up those slopes in her sandals, but now she heads downhill. First, the footpath across the heather, not purple yet but getting springy. The old sheep track is a fossil trace in her head. She veers back, across to the main track, stops to watch a young girl, about twelve years old, skip up from the mine road. She is wearing her school dress, her feet are bare.

'Where are your shoes, pet?'

'Don't need them.'

'Where are you going?'

The child waves towards the cottages on the hill, starts running towards them, over the tussock grass like a small deer, faster and faster.

She raises a hand to shade her eyes, but the girl has gone. Vanished. She scuffs at the stony track with her heel. It used to be like velvet, moss and sheep-nibbled grass, green as emeralds. A curlew calls, beak scything the sky. She walks back up the slope. This'll do, she thinks, for now. This'll last me for a bit. Her husband is still sitting in the folding chair by the side of the road in the heat. He shakes his head. He doesn't get it, obviously.

Chris Powell

Extract from Wallflower

The power of spring is waxing. One by one the wallflowers show their comeliness at last
in token that the winter months are past
Wallflowers – R H Forster

Donna early rising for the flower delivery, roses like dawn, coming in through the back yard, propping her bike against the wall, key in the door. A woman inside a woman, inside a woman, inside…and on like those Russian dolls, apple-cheeks, headscarves and fat flower bellies, an endless procession, a house of women, hands shaping, cutting, stitching, mending; weavers, dressmakers all, lives like beads strung on a thread, her heritage. Only now, weaving wire not silk and in *The Green Room*, her very own shop.

She thought of them still, the dolls, every time she opened up, did not forget, her mother Grace, her mother's mother Eva, her great grandmother Ellen. The lineage. As she ran the cold tap, refilled buckets, conditioned flowers, her fingers stiff with cold, they whispered in her ear mingling with breath in the sap fresh air. Eva cycling to Durham and back to fetch coupons for her wedding dress, Grace clocking-in, Astraka, Shildon, neck bent over sewing machine, cotton wool in her ears, feeding fake fur to the foot, needle through her finger; the baptism of women's work. Ellen, farmed out, sewing by oil lamp and cockroach. The women who went hungry first, gathered comfrey to stop the bleeding and mend the bones, on the move before the bond was due, colliery house, and a back yard of quarrel and clarts.

Women's lives, drops of rain on lady's mantle, her garden, keepers of dream. Her muslin christening bag, sewn by Eva, sugar, salt, candle, spice-cake – gone, a silver coin and the sprig of lavender, its scent lingering. Resilience, tenacity, risk. The risk: even if it folds tomorrow, if the customers dry up and let's face it there aren't that many customers, not yet. Even if it folds, she will not regret. They are waiting; all who've ventured to open up in Fore Bondgate, those already there, the Zairs, part of the town's history, clustered around a once village green, in an historic street.

'Be historic if you all go bust, if the visitors don't come. What's he done for the town anyway? Ruffer? Done nothing for the shops or the High Street,' the disbelievers, said. She'd given up trying to put them right, what did they expect? There were those who made an art of misery and complaint.

The things Donna loved about *The Green Room*: it was hers, all of it, trestle tables, jasmine hoops, out front setting up on the street, terracotta pots, seasonal bulbs, snowdrops, crocus. Looking back through the window to the interior, the bench salvaged from her grandfather's allotment shed, brown paper rolls and raffia, tissue and wild thyme candles, the way it smelled, the mirror above the chest on loan from Eva's house. Stems of eucalyptus, flowers.....

Hadn't she always loved flowers? Her favourite book, growing up, *The Secret Garden*. Dickon, good with animals and nature, like her Paul. Like most men, doesn't know a dandelion from a daisy, but it doesn't stop him believing. Once she got that City and Guilds, once he could see how good she was and what she dreamed of. Turned his hand to whatever he could, built it with her, at the weekends, the kids too, painting, brushes in hand. They'd all got the bug. The town, reimagined, forging future paths, the stretch from Green Room to Castle.

Walk with her in the low, copper, sun that warms the scaffold on the Castle stone, sets windows alight. Run your hands down the bark of the chestnuts, that grow by the river. Step up to the Deer House, remember that first kiss, a secret tryst. Know the gladness of entering that half-forgotten place you never meant to leave.

Avril Joy

The Wind from the Sierra

While researching my grandson's Spanish heritage,
I came across an old woman who as a girl had nursed
fighters in the Spanish Civil War.

In the twilight of the ward
the old woman pulls me to her side
she whispers in the tight shell of my ear.
Her voice, dancing on a roaring tide,
surfs sixty years of life
with West Coast ease.

I let down my hair, she says, when I
was nursing in the Spanish War.
After the lice, the blood, the mucus-mud
of that First Conflagration
many women cut their hair,
silky smooth to their skulls.
Not me! I treasured my locks.
Daytime on the ward I wore my hair
tightly bound, moulded to my head
like a Roman helmet. And every night
I brushed it out, tress by golden tress,
a miserly Rapunzel alone in my room.

Of course, I say, since that Spanish prelude
haven't we had our own wars here?
Not so much the innocence of fighting
face-to-face but cities raped, skies riven,
fire storms raging. Does this compare with
the Spanish cloth-capped anarchy all
fluttering flags and posters pitted innocently against
the tyranny of flying steel? Later
generations paid world rates for
learned arguments and justification -
the comfort men in suits. Little comfort
for hearts being ripped out of cities and of citizens,
when the price of planes and bombs
was paid in flesh and pain, and administered
by medallioned clerks.

In the twilight of the ward
the voice in my ear is now a fading tide
smelling of salt and iodine.
of Dettol and rotting fish.

My hair fell loose in Spain, she murmurs
I liked to feel it lifting
in the warm wind from the Sierra

Wendy Robertson

A Room with a (Lockdown) View

1.

The sun catches the spinning cowl on top of the chimney on the house opposite. From my first floor flat I look down on a road that's eerily quiet.

If I open my window and crane out I can see Mr Dashpandi, who runs the Asian Convenience Store on the corner of the street, chatting to a solitary customer while maintaining social distancing. It's rather comical, the two of them trying to communicate through face masks with excessive gesticulation.

The fruit and vegetables laid out on tables in front of the shop window look so bright and shiny – does he spend the evenings washing and polishing them I wonder?

The girl from downstairs is leaving for her daily jog attired in vibrant pink and grey lycra. A sight to lift the spirits – and the outfit's not bad either.

She's checking her Fitbit and off she goes, so it must be 10.30 am. She always leaves at 10.30 am, which means it's time for my coffee. What creatures of habit we are!

The couple in the upstairs flat are arguing again – sound carries in these converted terraced houses.

I was supposed to be going on holiday this week but lockdown has scuppered that. I wish I lived in the country, or just had a garden.

* * *

2.

My world has shrunk, it comprises a view of my garden framed by a window three feet by three feet. It is a pleasant view, the sparrows are clustering on the feeders and the shrubs are coming into bud. The daffodils have been out for a while now and I can see that the tulips are about to bloom.

Overhead, lapwings tumble in a cerulean sky and I can hear a woodpecker in the tree down by the byre – sound carries further in the silence.

Beyond the garden I can see the fells rising in serried ranks to the skyline. Dotted about are clusters of white sheep feeding on the grass. A quad bike is moving among them with a collie perched on the back.

He is my nearest neighbour, that farmer, and he lives over two miles away. I do miss seeing people. I miss popping down to the shops, having coffee and a pastry with my friends in the teashop.

The government is being rather draconian, I think, forcing everyone to self-isolate like this. Perhaps I should never have moved away from the city?

Mike Kane

The Nursing Home

The window of life can shut, close down
so desolate tears overflow
fight back
despair

time heals they say
can this be true?

Open the window, maybe a glimpse,
could there be joy?
Some light again?

Fight back
be brave

small steps they say
light will return.

Julia Organ

The Life Cycle of a Butterfly

A small tortoiseshell settled on the Michaelmas daisies. Nan nodded, as if I had just shown her something remarkable. 'Soon be looking for a warm place to hibernate', she said. Butterflies. There is an art to netting and releasing them unharmed. 'Imagine, me racing through the fields in a pair of Dad's old army shorts. People talked!' I released the brake on her wheelchair, we moved on.

The sex life of a butterfly is mysterious. Small tortoiseshells lay their eggs deep in the dark heart of nettle clumps. Their caterpillars are gregarious, they swing beneath the leaves in hammocks of finest silk and party all summer, until it is time to pupate.

When I knew her, Nan lived alone with her books. She gave me the mirror from her dressing table set, silver-rimmed, tortoiseshell backed. Sometimes when I pick it up it is Nan I see smiling back.

The small tortoiseshell chrysalis is camouflage coloured, dull, copper-washed lilac. The adult butterfly is so familiar we barely notice it until suddenly surprised by its bright wings and strings of iridescent blue pearls. Nan, reading her poetry on the radio, centre-stage in her own life at last.

It was a long autumn. The daisies faded. Nan's care home was closed to visitors. On a bright January day, I was allowed back. 'My spectacles don't work', she said. Last words, it turns out, and the lenses, I saw, were plain glass. A small tortoiseshell butterfly, lured out of hibernation by the false spring, struggled in the net curtains. I opened the window. There is an art to releasing them unharmed.

Chris Powell

The waiting room

I am in the waiting room. I've been in waiting rooms before, with tatty magazines or soothing goldfish tank. This waiting room is virtual. I am cocooned at home with my laptop, waiting to share coffee and discussion. We will wave at each other, note the décor of other people's rooms, hear the dog in the background. This is the new normal. But it is not the same. No subtle body language, no frisson of underlying tensions, no gentle banter. Welcome to Zoom. One day . . . I will be back in a real waiting room, waiting for real people.

Jo Cundy

Index to Photographs

Photography by Marie Gardiner & Lonely Tower Film and Media
www.lonelytower.co.uk
www.mariegardiner.co.uk